Grandpa's Perfect Plan

for R C Hill Students
Please enjoy!
Mrs. Zahller

Sue Zahller
Illustrated by Ayin Visitacion

To order additional copies of this book, contact:
Xlibris
1-888-795-4274
www.Xlibris.com
Orders@Xlibris.com

Amora and Grandma, her abuela, loved to bake. Many times that summer Grandma would suggest, "Let's bake a pie or cookies." But baking a chocolate cake was Amora's favorite. Sometimes they baked apple pie, which Grandpa, or abuelo, loved. He would come home from the library or having coffee with friends and there would be a freshly made pie, still warm and full of juicy love.

Amora lived with her grandparents on the south side of Chicago. The three of them had recently gone to an animal shelter. Grandma and Grandpa let Amora pick between several dogs to take home to help her feel less lonely.

Amora picked a 3-year old dog that was zippy, but not too much. Its coat was several colors and she fit easily on Amora's lap. Amora named her dog Zip. Little Zip was a licker with ears that fluttered when she walked, and good company for Amora while her parents were gone.

Amora's poppa had not been working for some time. He volunteered to join the U.S. Army last year. Being in the Army would provide money for his family but it also took him away to be a soldier. Amora was very proud of her poppa, yet she often felt sad from missing him.

Zip was a great comfort to Amora. Zip licking Amora made her giggle. When Amora giggled, Grandma and Grandpa would look at each other and feel good, too.

Amora's momma had been working. That was great until momma began coughing so much she wasn't sleeping well. Then she became too tired to work. Later she was too tired to be a good momma to Amora. Momma went to Aunt Sophia's house in Baltimore. Aunt Sophia has no children and always says she's "just crazy" about Amora. Baltimore has a special hospital Amora's momma could stay at named Johns Hopkins. Aunt Sophia would work, then visit her sister in the hospital and report about momma's health to Grandma and Grandpa.

While they were on the phone Amora stood close by to hear any news. While momma's doctors weren't sure when she would feel better, Amora was hopeful it would be soon.

She dreamt of the day when her poppa would be safe and her momma well again. Then the three of them would be back together as a family with their new dog, Zip!

Shortly after the school year began a phone call came from an
Army officer in Washington, D.C. Amora's poppa was injured!
He would be flown to a hospital in D.C. for surgery!

BALTIMORE, MD

WASHINGTON, D.C.

When Amora came home from school Grandma and Grandpa held her between them and explained what happened. Grandma asked would Amora like to bake with her so they might do something to stay busy. But Amora said, "Not now, abuela," and went to her room. With Zip she lay flat on her back looking at the ceiling. She was too sad and confused to talk. Zip was lying near Amora's feet but slowly inched her way up Amora's side to her chin and began licking.

Amora curled up into a donut shape and while thinking of her poppa began to sob, "Get well, please get well," over and over until she could cry no more and fell asleep.

Over the next few days Amora tried being a brave girl but it was so hard. She felt like she needed to see her parents for herself. She did not want more phone calls or reports. She told her abuelos: "We have to go and visit them and my hugs will make them better. We can do it. We'll find a way!"

Amora knew that money enough to fly to Washington, D.C. was like trying to catch a unicorn. They had no extra anything, especially money.

One afternoon about a week after the sad news, Grandpa was pacing back and forth in the living room. Suddenly he stopped. He suddenly gave out a big, "YES!"

Zip was so caught by surprise she sat up, ran around the kitchen in a frenzy, slipped on the tile floor and then slid on her side into the garbage can.

Grandpa was humming and tapping on the arm of his comfy chair waiting until Amora came home from school. Grandma was returning about the same time from the Piggly Wiggly with soup, or sopa, bones so Grandpa got them both to sit down at the same time. "Guess how we can make enough money to go see your parents, Amora?"

Amora looked first at Grandpa, then at Grandma. She was stumped. Grandpa then asked, "What are you two very good at together?" Grandma looked hard at Amora staring hard back at her.

Then they both reached out to grab each other's hands while laughing and shouted, "baking!!"

So Grandpa's plan was a bake fair! He spoke with the principal at Amora's school about hosting the sale in their large school gym. He spoke with the school's parent group about sending bake sale flyers home with each student. He asked if the parent group could provide volunteers to run the sale with the three of them. They all said, "We'd love to help!"

Meanwhile Amora and Grandma were super busy making their mouth-watering cakes, breads, cookies, brownies and pies to sell. The local newspaper ran a story and took their photo. Some readers sent in donations to help with airfare. Everyone was so kind!

Finally, Amora was ready to tell momma and poppa there was a way to come see them. Baltimore is close to D.C. so both parents could be seen. The doctors for her parents agreed both were well enough for a visit. Even Zip would travel in a carry-on crate!

Amora knew her get well wishes and Grandpa's perfect plan brought her straight to her parent's arms. While they weren't back home yet, that day was coming soon. The family knew the reason the bake sale was a huge success was because the main ingredient in the baking was love.

CPSIA information can be obtained
at www.ICGtesting.com
Printed in the USA
BVHW020952211118
533567BV00002B/17/P